MAPLE RIDGE

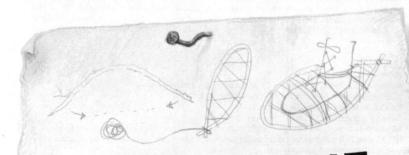

LOST IN THE
BLIZZARD

By Grace Gilmore
Illustrated by Petra Brown

LITTLE SIMON
NEW YORK LONDON TORONTO SYDNEY NEW DELHI

This book is a work of fiction. Any references to historical events, real people, or real places are used fictiously. Other names, characters, places, and events are products of the author's imagination, and any resemblance to actual events or places or persons, living or dead, is entirely coincidental.

 LITTLE SIMON

An imprint of Simon & Schuster Children's Publishing Division

1230 Avenue of the Americas, New York, New York 10020

This Little Simon edition December 2015

Copyright © 2015 by Simon & Schuster, Inc.

All rights reserved, including the right of reproduction in whole or in part in any form.

LITTLE SIMON is a registered trademark of Simon & Schuster, Inc., and associated colophon is a trademark of Simon & Schuster, Inc.

For information about special discounts for bulk purchases, please contact Simon & Schuster Special Sales at 1-866-506-1949 or business@simonandschuster.com.

The Simon & Schuster Speakers Bureau can bring authors to your live event. For more information or to book an event, contact the Simon & Schuster Speakers Bureau at 1-866-248-3049 or visit our website at www.simonspeakers.com.

Designed by Chani Yammer

The illustration of this book were rendered in pen and ink.

The text of this book was set in Caecilia.

Manufactured in the United States of America 1115 FFG

10 9 8 7 6 5 4 3 2 1

This book has been cataloged with the Library of Congress.

ISBN 978-1-4814-4750-8 (hc)

ISBN 978-1-4814-4749-2 (pbk)

ISBN 978-1-4814-4751-5 (eBook)

CONTENTS

A WALK IN THE FOREST

Logan Pryce paused on the wooded path and picked up a spindly branch.

"Nah, too skinny," he said to his dog, Skeeter.

Skeeter grabbed the branch with his teeth and gave a low, ferocious growl. He thought Logan was playing tug-of-war with him.

Logan's brother, Drew, turned

around. "What do you need a stick for, anyway?"

"It's for my new fix-it project," replied Logan.

"Wow, what are you fixing up?"

"It's a highly guarded secret. All shall be revealed soon!"

Drew rolled his eyes. Being a big brother, he rolled his eyes a lot.

Logan's new fix-it project was a sled! But he didn't want Drew to know because it was going to be a surprise for the whole family. Logan had found the broken old sled in the barn, and he had been tinkering with it in his Fix-It Shop. He needed some parts, like a few

sturdy branches and a length of strong rope. Winter was still a ways away, though, so he had plenty of time.

The two brothers continued down the path. Just a few weeks ago, the trees in the forest had been flush with gold and orange leaves.

5

Now they were bare and brown. A chill had settled in the air. Logan could feel it even through his wool cap, peacoat, and knickers.

Drew paused in front of a huge fallen tree. Something had knocked it down—maybe one of the big thunderstorms that had swept through Maple Ridge recently?

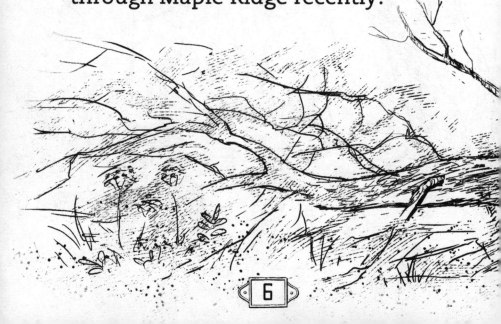

"This is a rock elm. These make for mighty good firewood. I wish I'd brought a saw," said Drew. Keeping the wood box full was one of his

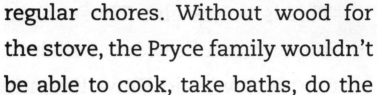

regular chores. Without wood for the stove, the Pryce family wouldn't be able to cook, take baths, do the laundry, or heat the house.

Logan glanced over his shoulder. Behind them on the path, he could see the sun

setting in the sky. "We should go," he told Drew.

Drew crouched down to inspect the fallen tree. "What are you afraid of, Logan? Getting lost in the dark, scary forest?" he joked.

"No!"

"We can stay a bit longer. I know these woods like the back of my hand. I could get us home in the pitch-black night with no lamp. Blindfolded, even."

That was another thing eleven-year-old brothers did a lot: *exaggerate*. It was a fit word for Drew, who liked to brag and boast about things he couldn't actually do.

"You can stay if you'd like. Skeeter and I are leaving now," Logan said with a shrug.

Drew sighed and stood up. "Oh, *fine*. I'd better come with you. I wouldn't want you to lose your way."

This time, it was Logan who rolled his eyes.

SHORTER DAYS

At dinner, Pa had news for the family.

"I've taken on some extra shifts at work. So I'll be in the city all weekend," he announced.

Pa used to be a farmer, but now he worked at a glass factory in Sherman. Sherman was two hours away by horse and buggy.

Tess raised her hand. "May I come with you, Pa? I so want to see the new Carnegie Library!" Tess, who was nine, loved to read. She always had her nose in a book.

"Oh, may I please come too, Pa? Mrs. Wigglesworth has never taken a trip to the big city!"

said four-year-old Annie. Mrs. Wigglesworth was a doll that Ma had sewn for her out of scraps.

Ma set a plate of biscuits on the table and sat down next to Pa. "Maybe another time, girls. Your pa will be busy working. Besides, I need you here to help with winterizing."

Logan grabbed two biscuits, then counted what was left: *One, two, three*. He pouted and put one back. "What's 'winterizing'?" he asked.

"It means getting ready for winter," said Tess.

"The first day of winter isn't until December twenty-first. That's a long ways away," Drew pointed out.

"Mother Nature doesn't keep her eye on the calendar, son. We have to

be prepared for harsh weather, no matter the date," Pa explained.

Drew considered this. Then he nodded and gave a little salute. "Leave it to me, Pa. I'll take care of things while you're away in Sherman. And I'll make sure the children stay out of trouble."

The children? Logan and Tess stared at Drew with gaping mouths.

Ma spooned roasted potatoes onto everyone's plates. "Where did you boys go after school, any- way? I thought, you were coming straight home."

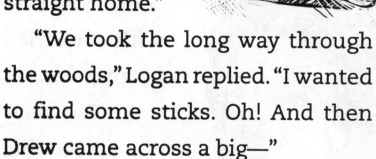

"We took the long way through the woods," Logan replied. "I wanted to find some sticks. Oh! And then Drew came across a big—"

"—deer! It sure did startle us!" Drew cut in.

Logan was confused. Why didn't Drew want to talk about the fallen rock elm? Ma and Pa would be glad to know about the extra firewood, especially with winter coming.

"Well, you know I don't like you kids roaming about when it's dark out," Ma said with a worried expression.

"The days are getting shorter," added Pa.

Logan gazed out the window. Pa was right. A month ago, they would have had plenty of daylight to play outside before supper. Now the sky was the color of ink. Wind rattled

the glass panes. Even with the oil lamp casting its warm golden glow, the kitchen seemed cold and dim.

"We promise we won't go roam-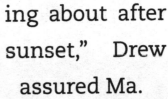ing about after sunset," Drew assured Ma.

Now it was Annie's turn to give a little salute. "Leave it to me, Ma and Pa. I'll make sure the children

stay out of trouble!" she said in a low, rumbly voice that sounded like Drew's.

Drew's cheeks flamed red. Everyone laughed.

CHAPTER 3

WHAT ABOUT THE SQUIRRELS?

On Friday, Pa left for work well before dawn. He took a small suitcase with him as well as a dozen jars of jam that Ma had packed for her sister, Violet. Pa would be staying with Violet and her family in their house in downtown Sherman.

After saying good-bye to Pa, Logan started in on his morning chores. As always, he had only a couple of hours to get everything done before school.

First, he went out to the hen-house to collect eggs. The chickens stopped laying eggs in winter, so it was important to enjoy them while they lasted. Pa had explained to him once that birds were aware of the seasons and laid eggs only in warmer weather.

Logan tackled the barn next. He had a lot of jobs to do there: mucking the stalls, milking the cows, and brushing the horses. Pa had taken Lightning

with him to Sherman, so there was only Buttercup to brush.

When Logan was finished, he dropped by his Fix-It Shop. The shop took up a stall in the corner of the barn. It consisted of a worktable, stool, and crates full of spare parts and tools.

30

On top of the worktable, under an old saddle blanket, was his secret sled project. Logan had already fixed a crack in one of the runners and sanded away the splinters. He rummaged through one

of the crates and found a piece of rope for the front of the sled.

"Hello? Logan? Are you in here?"

Logan quickly threw the blanket over the sled. Tess stood in the doorway. She glanced at Logan and the Fix-It Shop with a puzzled look.

"Ahoy there!" Logan said, trying to distract Tess with pirate talk.

"Can you help me haul water? Drew's busy chopping wood."

"Aye, matey!"

The two of them walked over to the well together and pumped cold water into buckets.

The sun was just begin-
ning to rise. Invisible
birds twittered noisily in
the bushes. In the gar-
den, vines sagged with
green tomatoes. The

leafy stems and white
tops of turnips peeked
out of the ground.

When Logan and

Tess brought the water back to the house along with fresh eggs and milk, their morning chores were done. Inside the kitchen, the delicious smells of breakfast greeted them. Ma stood at the stove, frying bacon with one hand and stirring porridge with the other. Annie sat cross-legged

on the floor, cranking the handle of a butter churn.

"Good morning, Logan! Good morning, Tess! I was telling Annie about the list Pa left us for tomorrow," said Ma.

"What jobs are on the list?" Tess asked curiously.

"Our winteriz- ing tasks. One, we need to harvest the garden and till the soil. Two, we need to pack jars of food and bring them to the root cellar to store. Three, we need to make sure the animals

have enough hay and feed. And four, we need to gather stones for Pa's new well house," Ma said, ticking off each item on her fingers.

"Winter sure is a lot of work," Logan mumbled.

"Oh, I *love* winter! Mrs. Wigglesworth and I are going to build a snowman family and have a tea party

with them!" Annie
said happily.

D r e w
strolled into
the kitchen
with an arm-
ful of logs.
He set them
down in a bin
next to the stove.
"You'd best be patient,
Annie. I predict we won't see
snow for another month!"

"But what about the squirrels?"
Tess piped up.

"What about them?" asked Drew.

"The squirrels have been running around like crazy, collecting acorns. They're burying them deeper too. I read in a book that it means a snowstorm is coming soon," Tess replied.

"Ha-ha," Drew scoffed.

As Logan dug into his porridge, he wondered who was right: Drew or the squirrels?

Just in case, I should finish up my sled project soon, he thought.

CHAPTER 4

• THE COMPASS •

At school, Miss Ashley had a surprise for all the students.

"Can anyone tell me what this is?" she asked. She held up a small object.

Logan leaned across his desk and squinted at the object. It was round and brass-colored, with a white face. He remembered seeing something like it at Mayberry's General Store, behind the glass case. It had been expensive—a whole dollar!

"Looks like a toy for babies!" Kyle Chambers hollered from the back of the room, where the older kids sat. Kyle's pal Lenny Watts guffawed.

Miss Ashley pursed
her lips. "No, Kyle, it's
not a toy. And we can
all hear you just fine."

"Perhaps a watch?"
Tess spoke up. She sat
in the middle of the

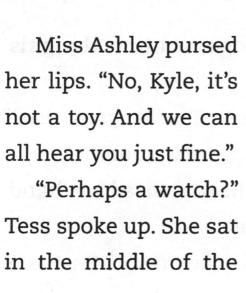

room, like Logan, but on the girls' side.

"That's close, Tess. Anyone else?" Miss Ashley peered around.

Anthony Bruna raised his hand. "It's a compass."

Miss Ashley beamed. "Yes, that's very good, Anthony!"

Logan patted Anthony on the shoulder.

"A compass is a device that can help us find our way," Miss Ashley explained. "It is aligned to a magnetic field that surrounds our planet."

Logan mulled this over. Back in the Fix-It Shop, he had a horseshoe-shaped magnet in his crate full of spare parts. He tried to imagine a bunch of them circling Earth. *How would that work?*

"When you hold the compass, this needle here tells you which way is north. Then you can find south, east, west—or somewhere in between, like northeast or south-west," Miss Ashley went on. "For example, if I hold the compass toward the door, it tells me that I'm facing south."

The class oohed and aahed.

"Each of you will take turns bringing the compass home. Your assignment will be to use the compass to figure out the direction points of your house—like front door, south;

back door, north. After everyone has done this, you will all make models of your houses with paper and glue. We will then combine our models to build a big map of Maple Ridge."

Models? A big map? Suddenly, this project sounded like a lot of fun to Logan!

"Who gets to take the compass home first?" Greta Kranz asked, patting the bow in her hair.

"We'll go in alphabetical order by last name. That means—" Miss Ashley glanced at her roll call list. "Anthony Bruna will be the first."

"Gosh, thanks, Miss Ashley!" Anthony said with a big grin.

After school, Logan caught up to Anthony in the schoolyard. The two of them had been best friends since they were little. A blustery wind had kicked up, and pine needles littered the ground. Logan didn't remember seeing them this morning.

Anthony dug into his pocket and pulled out the compass. He showed it to Logan.

"Isn't it swell?" he gushed. "See how the needle moves?"

The slender needle wobbled to N, for north. Anthony turned the compass to the right. The needle wobbled to E, for east.

"How does it know which way is which? Is it *magic*?" Logan said in wonder.

"Remember? Miss Ashley told us it was the magnetic feel . . . field . . . something like that. I'm going to ask Papa about it when he gets home from work. He's whip-smart about science."

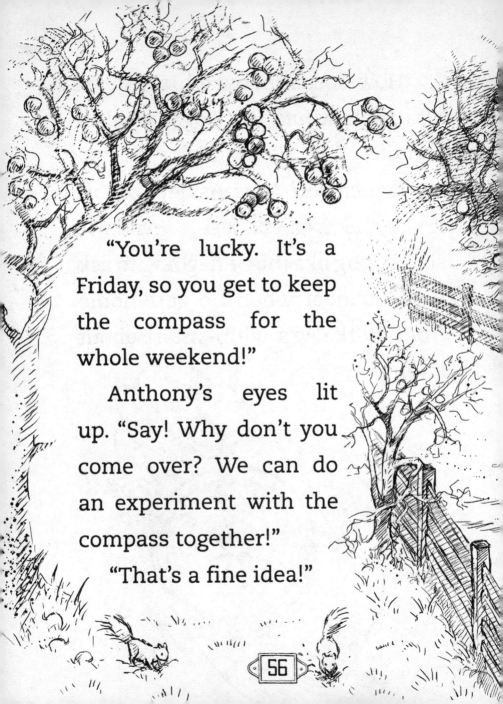

"You're lucky. It's a Friday, so you get to keep the compass for the whole weekend!"

Anthony's eyes lit up. "Say! Why don't you come over? We can do an experiment with the compass together!"

"That's a fine idea!"

They hurried down the road, eager to try out the magical new device. As they passed the Pritchetts' apple orchard, Logan noticed some squirrels digging furiously under a tree.

What were the squirrels up to?

CHAPTER 5

NORTH, SOUTH, EAST, WEST

At the Brunas', Logan and Anthony got busy mapping the house. Anthony pointed the compass this way and that while Logan took notes on a slate board. Mrs. Bruna was in the kitchen, chopping vegetables for a soup.

"The front door faces east . . . no, more like northeast!" Anthony

called out. "The back door faces south! The stove faces west! Papa's favorite rocking chair faces north!"

"I'm not sure if Miss Ashley cares about stoves and rocking chairs," Logan said with a laugh.

After they were done with the inside, they decided to map the barn, the smokehouse, and other outbuildings, just for fun.

Outside, the temperature had dropped, and Logan could see his breath in the air.

He inhaled and exhaled with as much force as he could muster. Anthony did the same. Together, they made a big, puffy cloud.

After making a few more breath clouds, Logan said, "Can I tell you a secret?"

"Sure!" replied Anthony.

"I'm making a sled in my Fix-It Shop!"

"Gosh, really? That is swell!

We'll be able to go sledding on Goat Hill this winter!"

Logan's eyes grew wide. Goat Hill was the biggest hill in Maple Ridge. Only the older kids sledded on it.

"Yup. Goat Hill," Logan said, trying to sound brave.

They walked around the yard, taking more measurements. The sun was starting to sink in the sky. When Anthony pointed the compass at the horizon, he saw that he was facing west. "Hmm. I guess the sun really does set in the west."

"That must mean the sun rises in the east and—" Logan stopped.

"Wait . . . *sunset!* I'd best be getting home. Ma says she doesn't want us roaming about after dark."

"You'd better go, then," Anthony agreed.

As they wound their way to the front yard, Mr. Bruna's buggy pulled up. The horse, Windsprite, nickered and pawed at the ground.

Mr. Bruna stepped out of the buggy and unhitched Windsprite. "Good evening, boys! What are you up to? Awful chilly to be playing outside."

"Logan was just leaving. Look, Papa!" Anthony said, showing him the compass. "Miss Ashley gave this to me for the weekend! It's the best homework assignment ever!"

"A compass, eh? You know, when I was a youngster, we used to make our own compasses with a bowl of water, a piece of wool, a needle, and a leaf," Mr. Bruna recalled. "See, you rub the needle with the wool. This creates a static charge.

When you
put the
needle
on the
leaf in
the water,
it will point
to the north."

"*Really?*" said Logan. This compass business really *was* magical.

"Speaking of compasses . . . do you boys know which way Windsprite is facing?"

Anthony held out the compass. "North, Papa!"

"That's right, Anthony. Animals don't like the wind in their faces, so they turn away from it. Windsprite is facing north, which means that the wind's blowing from the south. A wind from the south means a storm's coming."

"You mean . . . a rainstorm?" asked Logan.

"Actually, there's been talk about a snowstorm. Could even start tomorrow."

"A *snowstorm*?" Anthony gasped.

Logan thought about the squirrels. Perhaps they had been right after all!

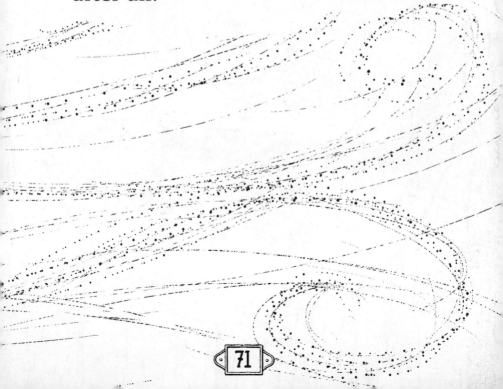

CHAPTER 6

PREPARING FOR WINTER

The next morning, Logan woke up to the sound of silence—no birds twittering outside.

He sat up in bed, pressed his face against the window, and flinched. The glass pane was ice cold, with a thin glaze of frost. Had that been there yesterday?

A snowstorm! he remembered.

But when he peered through the frost, he didn't see any snow. The trees and the ground were still brown. The air was crystal clear.

It's just as well, he thought. This way, he would have time to finish his sled project. Also, he and his family could do their winterizing.

Still, why were the birds so quiet?

Logan dressed quickly and went downstairs. Everyone was already in the kitchen. Ma was cooking pancakes and fried eggs. Tess was braiding Annie's hair. Drew was polishing his boots with an old rag. Skeeter was gnawing on a soup bone in front of the stove.

"Mr. Bruna said there will be a snowstorm this weekend," Logan announced. He plucked a pancake from the pan, dunked it in a pitcher of maple syrup, and stuffed the whole thing in his mouth.

"Logan Dale Pryce! *Manners!*"
Ma scolded him. "And what's this
about a snowstorm? How does
Mr. Bruna know?"

Logan chewed
quickly. "Um . . .
well . . . his horse
was facing
north."

"Ha!" Drew
scoffed. "That's
as bad as
Tess's balder-
dash about
the squirrels."

"It's not balderdash. It was in a book!" Tess said hotly.

"Does 'balderdash' mean that you're bald?" Annie asked curiously.

"It means 'nonsense.' Everyone, please! Let's eat up so we can get to work. Snow or not, we have a lot of chores to get through today," said Ma.

A short while after breakfast, the five Pryces had bundled up and headed outside.

They started working in the garden. Ma explained that it was important to harvest the remaining fruits and vegetables, since a hard frost could destroy them. Most of them would be canned and eaten over the long winter. Some, like the potatoes, could simply be stored in wooden barrels. The green tomatoes would be wrapped in newspaper to ripen in the root cellar.

They worked steadily for the next few hours, even Annie, whose job was to brush dirt and soil from the potatoes. As the morning

progressed, Logan noticed puffy gray clouds gathering low in the sky. The air felt heavy and damp, even though it wasn't raining.

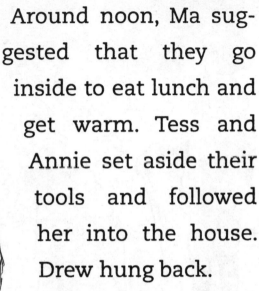

Around noon, Ma suggested that they go inside to eat lunch and get warm. Tess and Annie set aside their tools and followed her into the house. Drew hung back.

"Aren't you going in?" Logan asked Drew.

"In a minute. I've been meaning to go back for that old tree," replied Drew. "I want to surprise Ma and Pa with some extra firewood."

Logan nodded slowly. So *that's* why Drew had kept quiet about the fallen tree the other night!

"Do you want me to help you? I'm pretty good at hauling heavy things," Logan offered.

"Nah. This is grown-up stuff. You should stay here and have lunch with the ladies—or maybe play with your little secret invention."

Lunch with the ladies? Little secret invention?

"Fine! I hope you drop a log on your toe!" Logan huffed.

Drew rolled his eyes, picked up a saw, and headed toward the forest.

CHAPTER 7

● WHITEOUT! ●

Ma, Tess, Annie, and Logan had just finished their lunch when Skeeter began to bark.

"What is it, boy?" Logan asked.

Skeeter pointed his nose at the kitchen window and continued barking. Everyone turned.

They saw a white flake . . . then another . . . then another.

"*Snow!*" Logan shouted.

"I knew it! The squirrels were right!" exclaimed Tess.

"Hooray! Mrs. Wigglesworth and I can have our tea party with the snowman family!" Annie added.

"My goodness! I'm glad we finished with the garden. We can tackle the rest of

the items on Pa's list another time."
Ma paused and glanced around.
"Where's Drew?"

"Um . . ." Logan
scrambled to come up
with an explanation.
He was still mad at
Drew, but he didn't
want to ruin the
firewood surprise.
"He . . . um . . .
went to the barn
to check on the
animals. I'll go fetch
him!"

Before Ma could ask any more questions, Logan pulled on his coat, gloves, and cap, and raced out

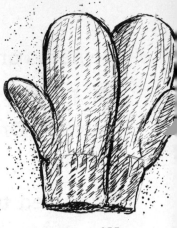

the door with Skeeter. *First, I'll find Drew. Then I'll help him carry the firewood back to the house,* he thought.

On the way to the forest, Logan stopped by the barn and grabbed his sled. It wasn't completely finished, but it might come in handy.

He also brought his
walking sticks and
some snowshoes
that he had made
last year out of
wood, wire, and
leather scraps.

Logan hurried toward the forest, dragging the sled behind him. The snow was coming down harder now, and the landscape was quickly turning from brown to white. An icy wind whipped around.

At the edge of the forest, Logan yelled: *"Drew!"*

There was no answer.

Frowning, Logan tried to remember the location of the rock elm tree. Was it to the right or the left or straight ahead? Drew was likely there, waiting out the sudden storm.

And then he remembered. On

Thursday, he and Drew had been traveling from west to east through the forest. He knew this because he'd looked over his shoulder to see the sun setting behind him, and the sun always set in the west!

If only he could figure out which way was west. He needed a compass.

Crack! A small tree limb landed softly. Pine needles were laid out against the snow.

"Needles! That's it! We'll make our own compass!" he told Skeeter.

Logan checked his jacket pocket for the needle he kept there to pin his mittens. He would use his cap for the wool. He soon found a leaf, and all he needed was some water.

But where would he find water in the middle of a snowstorm?

LOGAN TO THE RESCUE

Logan began kicking at the snow. Maybe there was a puddle hiding underneath all that white.

Skeeter was eager to join the game. He pawed at the snow and sent it flying into the air.

They did this for a while—Logan kicking, Skeeter digging.

Slurp, slurp, slurp.

Logan whirled around. Skeeter was lapping water from a puddle!

"Good boy, Skeeter!" shouted Logan. Luckily, the puddle wasn't frozen yet, and there was enough water in it to cobble together a compass.

He took off his wool cap and rubbed the needle against it, just like Mr. Bruna had described. Then he carefully laid the needle on the leaf in the water. He leaned over the puddle to protect it from the wind and snow.

The leaf floated slightly. Slowly, gradually, it began turning like the handle of a clock. After a minute, it settled and became still.

"Skeeter, that's north!" Logan said, pointing. "That means west is *that* way! We did it, boy!"

Skeeter's honey-colored tail whipped back and forth happily.

There was no time to waste. Logan began stomping westward with his snowshoes and his sled. Skeeter trotted alongside him.

Now the snow was falling almost sideways. It stung Logan's eyes and made it impossible to see. He shielded his face with his hand and inched forward step by step.

Just keep going west, he told himself.

After what seemed like forever, he stopped in his tracks and glanced around. Nothing but white.

"Drew!" he yelled again.

"*Logan!*" came a voice from a distance.

Relief washed over Logan. He'd found his brother!

"Drew! Keep talking so I can find you! Or sing a song!"

After a moment, Drew began singing:

> "*In the snowing and the blowing*
> *In the cruelest sleet*
> *Little flow'rs begin their growing*
> *Far beneath our feet*"

Logan moved toward the voice. Another thirty steps more . . . and he spotted the fallen rock elm.

Drew sat huddled under a shelter of elm branches, next to a pile of freshly cut logs.

"Drew!"

"Logan!" Drew jumped up and gave him a fierce hug. "Am I ever glad to see you! Thanks a bunch for finding me!"

Logan smiled to himself. Drew had never hugged him before.

"You're welcome! Let's load the firewood onto my sled and get home quick. Ma's probably wondering where we are. You can borrow my snowshoes."

"You mean those ugly stick things on your feet? I'm fine with just my boots," said Drew.

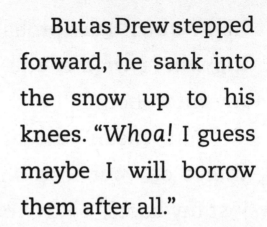

But as Drew stepped forward, he sank into the snow up to his knees. "*Whoa!* I guess maybe I will borrow them after all."

Logan unstrapped his snowshoes and handed them to Drew.

"Thanks again," Drew said sheepishly.

"You're welcome again."

"Say, is that your secret project? The sled?"

"Yup."

"Huh. It's pretty nifty!"

For the first time, Logan didn't feel like such a little brother.

CHAPTER 9

⊕FUN IN THE SNOW⊕

By Sunday morning, the storm had passed. Glistening white snow blanketed all of Maple Ridge.

Ma gave Logan and Drew permission to go sledding, even though she was still upset at them for worrying her during the blizzard. When they'd finally made it back to the house, she'd hugged and scolded

them at the same time. Fortunately, she'd been pleased about the new firewood. She, Tess, and Annie had admired Logan's sled, too.

Over at Goat Hill, everyone in town seemed to be out: sledding, cross-country skiing, building forts,

making snow angels, and having snowball fights. Logan spotted Anthony, Wally Robbins, and a
bunch of other kids from school.

Anthony ran up to him. "Ahoy there! What do you think of all this powdery stuff?" he called out cheerfully.

"It's pretty grand! I brought my new sled and my snowshoes, too!" said Logan.

"Could I borrow your snowshoes? I've been keen to try them. And then maybe we could take a run on your new sled?"

"Aye, matey!"

Logan handed the snowshoes to Anthony and showed him how to strap them on. Anthony thanked him and stomped toward his parents and his little sister, Isabella, who had just arrived. Ma had said she would be by later too, with Tess and Annie.

"Hey, Logan! Let's go sledding!"

Logan turned around.

Drew was waving him over from the base of the hill. "Come on, what are you waiting for?"

Logan glanced anxiously at the top of the hill. The steep slope had frightened him ever since he was little.

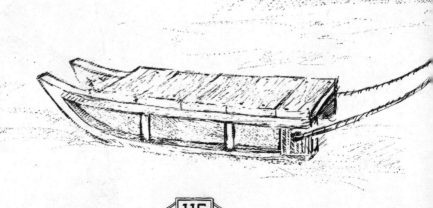

On the other hand, a lot of kids were sledding down it, and they looked as though they were having a perfectly fine time.

Logan took a deep breath. Maybe the hill wasn't as big and scary as he remembered.

He pulled his sled over to Drew. The two brothers started up the hill together.

"I think you should be the pilot, don't you?" Drew suggested.

"Aye, matey!"

Drew gave Logan a salute. Logan saluted back.

It was going to be a long, fun winter.

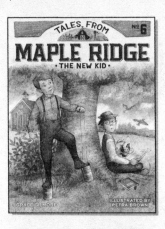

Check out the next

TALES FROM MAPLE RIDGE

adventure!

HERE'S A SNEAK PEEK!

Logan Pryce yawned as he started up the hill toward the Maple Ridge School with his older brother, Drew, and older sister, Tess. He had woken up before dawn to help Pa chop wood.

Tess was chattering about birds when the three of them reached the crest of the hill. She could be shy

at times, but not when it came to things she cared about, like books and birds.

Drew leaned over to Logan. "If I have to hear any more about birds, I'm going to stick my head in the ground like an ostrich," he joked.

"Or you could flap your arms like a goose and fly away!" Logan joked back.

The two brothers chuckled.

Up ahead was their one-room schoolhouse. A thin column of smoke rose from the chimney. The trees in the yard were cloaked with red and yellow leaves.

Logan spotted Kyle Chambers and Lenny Watts strolling through the door with their lunch pails. And then he spotted a boy he didn't recognize. The boy was as tall and skinny as a beanpole. He wore oval-shaped, gold-rimmed glasses and an odd hat decorated with a feather.

Exactly twenty students attended the Maple Ridge School, and Logan knew every single one.

Except for this boy. Who was he?